6/98 ⑰
9/99 ㉚

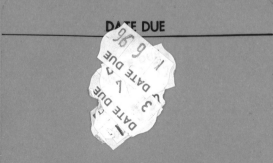

And Then What?

by **JAKE WOLF**

pictures by
MARYLIN HAFNER

Hi!

Greenwillow Books
NEW YORK

Watercolors, colored pencil, and pen and ink were used for the full-color art.
The text type is ITC Veljovic Medium.

Printed in Hong Kong by South China Printing Company (1988) Ltd.
First Edition   10   9   8   7   6   5   4   3   2   1

Library of Congress Cataloging-in-Publication Data

Wolf, Jake
   And then what? / by Jake Wolf; illustrated by Marylin Hafner.
      p.   cm.
   Summary: Willy and his mother discuss how he will spend the
day and night, including a sail to France in a trash basket.
   ISBN 0-688-10285-9 (trade). ISBN 0-688-10286-7 (lib.)
   [1. Imagination — Fiction.   2. Mothers and sons — Fiction.]
I. Hafner, Marylin, ill.   II. Title.
PZ7.W81913An   1993   [E] — dc20   90-24644   CIP   AC

FOR CHELSEA—
NO BONES ABOUT IT
— J. W.

FOR KATHERINE S.,
WITH LOVE
— M. H.

Willy and his mother were having lunch in the coffee shop.

"We have a lot of things to do this afternoon," said his mother.

"What are we going to do?" said Willy.

"Well," said his mother,
"we'll go to the market
and get some groceries."
"And then what?" said Willy.

"We'll get some apples
at the fruit stand."
"And then what?" said Willy.

"We'll go to the cleaners
and pick up Daddy's suit."
"And then what?" said Willy.

"We'll go to the card shop
and get a birthday card
for Grandma."
"And then what?" said Willy.

"Then we'll take the bus home," said his mother.

"And then what?" said Willy.

"Well," said his mother,
"we'll put away the groceries,
and we'll hang Daddy's suit
in the closet."
"And then what?" said Willy.

"We'll pile the apples on a plate,
and we'll send the birthday card
to Grandma."
"And then what?"

"You'll have supper when Daddy comes home."

"And then what?"

"It will be time for your bath."

"And then what?"

"You'll get ready for bed."

"And then what?"

"We'll read a book together."

"And then what?"

"I'll say, 'Good night, Willy,' and I'll close
 your door so you can sleep."
"And then what?"

"You'll go to sleep."
"But what if I can't? Then what?"
 said Willy.

"Well," said his mother,

"let me think."

"Tell me," said Willy.

"You'll look out your window.

 It will be dark."

 "And then what?"

"You'll clap your hands
   together, and all the stars
   will come out."
"And then what?"
"You'll say, 'Shush,'
   and the whole city
   will be silent."
"And then what?"

"You'll whisper, 'Snow,' and snow will start to fall."

"And then what?"

"It will snow until it reaches
    your window."
"And then what?"

"You'll say, 'I didn't mean
    that much.'"
"And then what?"

"The sun will come out,
  and the snow will melt."
 "And then what?"
 "The streets will be rivers."
 "And then what?"
 "You'll sail around the city
  in a trash basket
  with an umbrella
  for a sail."
 "And then what?"
 "You'll stop at your friends'
  houses and say, 'Want a ride?'"
 "And then what?"

"Betty will say, 'Okay,'

and Joey will say, 'Sure,'

and Loretta will say, 'Can I bring my dog?'"

"And then what?"

"You'll sail past
Daddy's office
and say, 'Hello.'"
"And then what?"
"You'll sail away…
and away…
and away."
"And then what?"

"You'll come to France
and see your cousin Rose.
She'll say, 'Bonjour.'"
"And then what?"
"She'll throw you
little pastries for the
trip back home."
"And then what?"

"Halfway home, a big wind
   will come."
 "And then what?"
"The wind will pick up your
   umbrella and carry you
   toward the city."
 "And then what?"

"The wind will stop."

"And then what?"

"The umbrella will fall."

"And then what?"

"A spider will come down and
   say, 'Would you like a bridge
   to the city?'"
"And then what?"
"You'll say, 'Yes, please,' and
   the spider will spin one."
"And then what?"

"Betty will slide to her house,
and Joey will slide to his house,
and Loretta and her dog
will slide to their house."
"And then what?"

"I don't know, Willy," said Willy's mother.

"I just don't know…"

"I know!" said Willy.

"You do?" said Willy's mother.

"I'll come home to you!" said Willy.